P9-DXG-665

CALGARY PUBLIC LIBRARY

DEC   2015

SEALED WITH A KICK

adapted by Maggie Testa

Simon Spotlight

New York   London   Toronto   Sydney   New Delhi

SIMON SPOTLIGHT
An imprint of Simon & Schuster Children's Publishing Division
1230 Avenue of the Americas, New York, New York 10020
This Simon Spotlight edition December 2015
Kung Fu Panda Legends of Awesomeness © 2015 Viacom International Inc.
All Rights Reserved.
NICKELODEON and all related logos are trademarks of
Viacom International Inc. Based on the feature film "Kung Fu Panda"
© 2008 DreamWorks Animation LLC. All Rights Reserved.
All rights reserved, including the right of reproduction in whole or
in part in any form.
SIMON SPOTLIGHT, READY-TO-READ, and colophon are
registered trademarks of Simon & Schuster, Inc.
For information about special discounts for bulk purchases, please contact
Simon & Schuster Special Sales at 1-866-506-1949 or
business@simonandschuster.com.
Manufactured in the United States of America 1115 LAK
2 4 6 8 10 9 7 5 3 1
ISBN 978-1-4814-1749-5 (hc)
ISBN 978-1-4814-1748-8 (pbk)
ISBN 978-1-4814-1750-1 (eBook)

Po was visiting his father at the
noodle shop one afternoon when he
noticed a crowd in the street.
Po went to see what was going on.
Four dancers were performing
right outside!

Po's father was excited for new customers.
Po was excited to watch the dancers.
He thought their moves were totally awesome.

After the show was over, Po
introduced himself to the dancers.
"It's a great honor to be
in your presence,
Dragon Warrior," said Su,
their leader.

Su introduced the other dancers.
One of them was named Song.
Song asked Po if he would take her
on a tour of the village.
"I would love to," said Po.

Song and Po had a great day
together.
Song wanted to give Po
something to say thank you.

It was a picture of a heart.

Then Po showed Song how his butt is shaped like a heart!

The more time Song spent with Po,
the more she liked him.
"There's something I need to tell
you," Song began.
"You can tell me anything," said Po.
"We're like best friends now."
But before Song had a chance to
speak, Su and the other
dancers arrived.

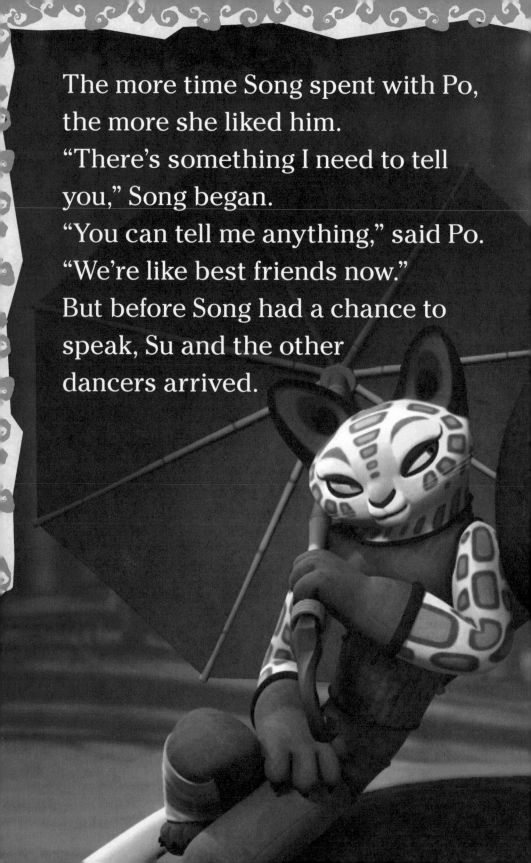

"Did you ask him?" Su asked Song.
"Ask me what?" said Po.
"We have no place to stay,"
Su told him.

"I am the Dragon Warrior," Po said.
"My job is to help people.
You are all invited to stay
at the Jade Palace."

Back at the Jade Palace, the dancers
put on a show for Po and the Furious
Five. But it was all just a trick
to steal Shifu's dragon chalice!

The chalice was a tall
white-and-gold cup that
Oogway had given
to Shifu to protect.
Po and the Furious Five weren't
going to let them get away with it!

The kung fu warriors were closing in as the dancers huddled together. Smoke poured out of their umbrellas and filled the Jade Palace. Po and the Furious Five couldn't see and the dancers got away!

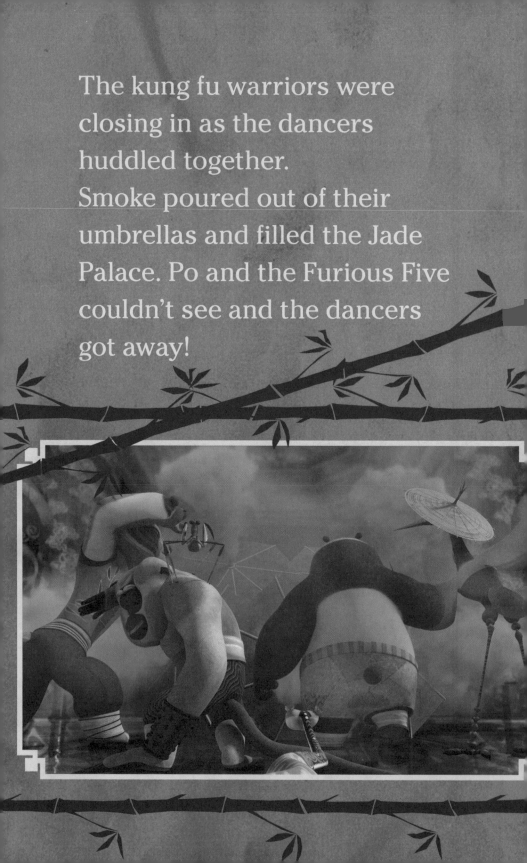

"Nice work, Po!" shouted Tigress.
"What were you thinking?"
"They said they needed a place
to stay," replied Po.
"They lied to you," said Crane.
"They only wanted to steal
the chalice."

Po, Viper, and Mantis went off to find the dancers and the chalice before Shifu discovered that it was missing.

They followed the dancers' trail
through the Canyon of the Shrieking
Wind.
The wind picked them up and
dropped them in front of the
dancers' hideout.
A guard stood at the door. Po dressed
up as a dancer to fool him!

Po's disguise worked!
As soon as he
was inside the hideout, he saw the
dragon chalice.

But the dancers weren't going to
give it up without a fight.

Po told Viper and Crane to take the
chalice and fly away.
He would see them back at the canyon
The chalice was safe,
but now Po had to fight alone.

The dancers threw everything they
had at him, including tiny, sharp
umbrellas.
Song could see that Po needed help.
"I heard you could use a friend,"
she told him.

Together, Po and Song raced out of the hideout and back toward the Canyon of the Shrieking Wind.

The dancers were about to catch up to them when Po heard the familiar sound of the wind rushing through the canyon.

Po had an idea.
"Close your umbrella,"
he told Song just before
the wind picked up.

It carried the other dancers away!

Su landed against a big rock.
Crane and Viper tied her up.
She wouldn't be stealing from anyone
again for a long time.

Po turned to Song. "What do you say you and I head back to the Valley of Peace?" he asked her.

But Song had other plans.
"I was thinking the dancers need a
new leader," she said.
"Someone that can
get them
away from a life of crime."

"I'd love to," said Po. "But I have a lot on my plate right now as the Dragon Warrior."

Song smiled. "I was talking about me," she said.

And then she kissed Po good-bye!

Po returned to the Jade Palace just as Shifu walked in.

"Has anyone seen the dragon chalice?" Shifu asked.

Po handed it to Shifu.

And that's when Shifu noticed something on the rim of the chalice.

"Is that lipstick?" he asked.